BLT

Play Pretend

Celebrating friendship,
creativity, and the magic
of make-believe

The Adventures of BLT - BLT Play Pretend
Author: Allison Hoppe
Illustrations: Tabassum Hashmi
Creative Director: David Murack
Interior Layout: Emily Strozinsky
Project Coordinator: Brenda Cortez
Art Coordinator: Jean Sime

ISBN: 979-8-9908071-0-5

Published by Pretty Lake Productions, LLC
Printed in China

To my favorite people:

Brooklyn, Lucy, & Theo

My heart and these books are all for you. A huge thank you to my cousin and creative partner, David Murack. None of this would be possible without you and I'm forever grateful. And to everyone who believed in The Adventures of BLT: THANK YOU!

Brooklyn Bacon, Lucy Lettuce, and Theo Tomato are best friends. Every day they go on wonderful adventures together.

Their imaginations run wild, and you
never know what they will come up with next!

• • •

But no matter what, they always have

the best time!

Today was an exciting day:

BLT went to the park to play pretend!

• • •

"What do you want to be when you grow up?" asked Theo.

They all took a moment to think.

"I want to be a superhero!" said Brooklyn.

"I will have a cape and fly around saving people!

• • •

Never fear!
Brooklyn Bacon
is here!"

"Earth sure does look pretty from up here! Flying in the sky is the perfect place to keep an eye out for trouble," said Brooklyn.

Brooklyn was flying around, when she got an alert that two sightseers on a safari trip were in danger!

• • •

"Duty calls!"

B

“Look! There’s a giant elephant coming your way!”

warned Brooklyn.

• • •

“Watch out or you’re going to get crushed!”

Brooklyn soared into the sky, flying over to Lucy and Theo.

"Hold on everyone,

I'll fly us away from here!"

she said.

“That was fun!”

said Lucy.

• • •

They all giggled and laughed.
“You’ll make a great superhero!” smiled Theo.

“I’m going to be a Pirate!”

shouted Lucy.

• • •

“I’ll have a big ship and sail the sea looking for gold!”

“I’m Captain
Lucy Lettuce!

Time to set sail!”

"Arrr Mateys! The sea is smooth,
and the air smells fresh!

Shiver me timbers!
Look, I see an island!

Hold tight everyone, and keep your
good eye out for sea monsters!"

• • •

"Aye Aye, Captain Lucy!"

shouted Brooklyn and Theo.

“Prepare to anchor!”

They anchored on the island and started digging.

"I found the treasure chest!"
screamed Brooklyn.

They opened the chest to find shiny gold and excitedly threw the coins into the air.

“You’ll be the best pirate that
ever sailed the sea.” said Brooklyn.

“What about you
Theo? What do you
want to be?”

asked Lucy.

“I want to be a Cowboy!

I’m going to live on a range, own a ranch, and round up cattle. You can call me Ranger Theo Tomato!

• • •

Yeehaw!”

“What a beautiful day on the ranch. Today I need to feed the chickens, haul the hay, tend to the garden, and round up the cattle.” said Theo.

Theo started his morning chores and noticed that two cows were walking off the ranch.

• • •

“Hey you two, you can’t leave the ranch!”

Theo hopped on his horse to ride after the cattle.

“I see two cattle in front of me that need rounding up!”

• • •

Brooklyn and Lucy looked at each other and said, “You’ll never catch us!” and started running away.

“Be careful so you don’t fall off your horse!” shouted Lucy.

He twirled his rope in the air and released it.

“Yes! I caught you two!”

Theo said, “Thanks for letting me practice my cowboy skills!”

• • •

“You’ll make a great cowboy one day.”

said Lucy.

“That was a great game!”

laughed Brooklyn.

“I really hope we get to be
a superhero, pirate, and cowboy
when we grow up!”

Theo shouted.

“As long as we are together,
we can do anything!”

said Lucy.

They put their hands together and chanted...

• • •

BLT! BLT! BLT!

BLT
BLT
BLT

B
!
Find BLT & Friends
The adventure continues! Help to
find BLT and their friends that are lost
at the ranch, on a safari, and at sea!

about the author

Allison Hoppe is the author of *The Adventures of BLT.* Her work is inspired by her nieces and nephew, Brooklyn, Lucy, & Theo. When Allison is not writing, she is going on adventures with the real BLT, traveling, learning, and ever-evolving.